DESIGN for Maximum Impact

Dear Reader

When I am writing my books, I think about how I would like to design each page so that they're interesting for you to read. This book has been a pleasure to write because there are many ideas about how to design all kinds of things with maximum impact.

DESIGN SHOULD NEVER SAY 'LOOK AT ME'. IT SHOULD ALWAYS SAY 'LOOK AT THIS'.

In Chapter 7, we provide you with a persuasive argument for the design value of a manual toothbrush over an electric toothbrush. Which do you use?

Chapter 5 explains some of the principles of designing clothes for kids and designing a children's clothing store.

I hope the ideas provide you with inspiration for your own projects.

Sharon Parsons

NELSON
CENGAGE Learning™
For learning solutions, visit **cengage.com.au**

Contents

DESIGN for Maximum Impact

1 Designing for Maximum Impact

Think about something you use that has a major impact upon you and your life. Everyone will think of something different. Some people may nominate their smartphone because they can use it to conveniently access the internet, instant messages, music and games. People working in extremely cold climates, like Antarctica, may regard a warm, strong building that withstands freezing blizzards as having a major impact on their lives. Astronauts working in a zero-gravity space station may choose pressure suits. And people living in a remote village in a developing country may say a new system that provides clean, uncontaminated drinking water is crucial to their lives.

What's important to me?
You can't beat ... oops, hang on, I've just received a text!

What's important to me?
You can't beat a strong building to stay warm in!

What's important to me?
You can't beat a good pressure suit to stay safe in!

What's important to me?
Wondering when it's going to be my sister's turn to work this pump!

What's important to me?
You can't beat a clean, safe supply of drinking water!

MINIATURE

Wooden screws were designed and used as early as 100 BCE, but it wasn't until the 1700s that an efficient process for making metal screws was designed.

MEDIUM

Mobile phone design has changed immensely since the first model, which appeared in 1973. It weighed around one kilogram, and cost US$3995

MASSIVE

With the power to carry over 400 tonnes, giant mining trucks are designed for heavy work. Their tyres are over 4 metres tall and weigh more than 5 tonnes each.

MONOLITHIC

Some archaeologists think Egypt's pyramids were designed to represent the descending rays of the Sun. Interior passages were designed to face particular stars.

MONUMENTAL

Legend has it that the czar Ivan the Terrible liked Moscow's St Basil's Cathedral so much, he blinded the designer so he'd never design a better building!

MEMORABLE

Gustave Eiffel's design for the Eiffel Tower was initially met with much resistance from Parisians who felt it would ruin the city's skyline!

2 Design Changes Over Time

Designing is the process of taking an idea and, using technical knowledge and creativity, preparing a plan to create a product, a process or a system. Physical factors, such as technology and materials, and social factors, such as the requirements of users (or consumers), are important considerations in design.

Designing in Prehistoric Times

Designing is a basic human activity. Since prehistoric times, people have been finding ways to use the materials around them to improve their lives. As materials, technology and knowledge have changed, so too have design solutions. Many of our needs and desires are the same as they were 40 000 years ago, but the things designed to satisfy them have undergone change over time.

A Sustainable Design
Hey, I've just designed a self-propelling bio-vehicle that runs on grass and water. Soon, everyone will be driving one!
That's all very well, but what happens when we run out of grass? Why not design a vehicle that runs on oil? There are plentiful supplies of oil.
An Unsustainable Idea
Consumer Needs Change
Oh-oh, looks like the time is right to design a circular rolling device. I think I'll call it something catchy, like a "wheel"!

The Evolution of Design

HUMAN NEED: TO BUILD STRUCTURES FOR SHELTER

Design 1 (Early Civilisations)

Need for Change: Scarcity of natural protection from the elements and predators, requirement for temporary structures to suit nomadic lifestyle

Materials and Technology: Natural materials found in immediate environment, unprocessed

Design Solution: Simple reed and branch structures

a reed house in South America

a brick, timber and tile house in Europe

Design 2 (Middle Ages)

Need for Change: Necessity of more permanence to suit settled lifestyle

Materials and Technology: Natural materials processed into bricks, timber and tiles

Design Solution: Permanent structures

a skyscraper in Dubai

Design 3 (Now)

Need for Change: Scarcity of energy, scarcity of available land, requirement for maximum comfort

Materials and Technology: Natural and artificial resources, processed into durable, environmentally responsible materials

Design Solution: Contemporary "green" building of multiple storeys, to maximise available land

The Evolution of Design

HUMAN NEED: TO PROVIDE PROTECTION AND COMFORT FOR FEET

woven flax shoes from Russia

Design 1 (Early Civilisations)

Need for Change: Requirement for protection and comfort

Materials and Technology: Natural materials found in immediate environment, unprocessed

Design Solution: Simple tied flax wraps, leather moccasins

Design 2 (Middle Ages)

Need for Change: Requirement for fashion, as well as practicality

Materials and Technology: Natural materials, processed and extensively worked

Design Solution: More complex fashion-driven leather shoes

leather Medieval-style shoes

Design 3 (Now)

Need for Change: Requirement for fashion and enhanced sports performance

Materials and Technology: Natural and artificial resources, processed into durable, environmentally responsible materials

Design Solution: Contemporary running shoes

a twenty-first-century running shoe

The **Evolution** of **Design**

HUMAN NEED: TO TRANSPORT PEOPLE AND GOODS

a donkey and cart

Design 1 (Early Civilisations)

Need for Change: Limitations of travelling by foot

Materials and Technology: Animals, for example horses and donkeys

Design Solution: Carts

Design 2 (Nineteenth Century)

Need for Change: Requirement for speed and less feeding and maintenance

Materials and Technology: Metal, wood, fuel

Design Solution: Early automobiles

an 1885 Benz automobile

Design 3 (Now)

Need for Change: Safety, even more speed, fuel efficiency and maximum comfort

Materials and Technology: Lightweight alloys, improved engines, composite materials

Design Solution: Contemporary automobiles

a sleek twenty-first-century sports car

The Evolution of Design

HUMAN NEED: TO FIND AN EFFECTIVE, HUMAN-POWERED MODE OF TRANSPORT

a penny-farthing

Design 1 (Nineteenth Century)

Need for change: Requirement for cheaper alternatives to automobiles

Materials and Technology: Steel, wood, leather

Design Solution: Penny-farthing bicycle

Design 2 (Twentieth Century)

Need for Change: Requirement for improved comfort as well as practicality

Materials and Technology: Steel, leather, rubber

Design Solution: Bicycles with improved tyres, seating and accessibility

a 1970s bicycle

Design 3 (Now)

Need for change: Requirement for speed and improved performance

Materials and Technology: Lightweight alloys, rubber, composite plastics, carbon fibre

Design Solution: Contemporary bicycles for racing, transport and recreation

a twenty-first-century road-racing bicycle

3 Impact Designs = Ideas and Designers

Designing anything for maximum impact starts with great ideas. A designer or team of designers must possess a multitude of creative and technical skills to take those ideas and use them to create a product or service that fulfils a need.

Designers are involved in virtually every aspect of society, through their input into products, buildings, services and virtually every form of communication. A good designer needs to possess several attributes: he or she must be multi-skilled, up-to-date with design software, be able to juggle many requirements at once and have a good understanding of different industries and the needs of consumers. Above all, a designer needs to be able to think and work in creative and practical ways to produce solutions that fulfil a need as specified in a design brief and within an agreed budget.

a graphic designer at work

Designers = Problem Solvers

Essentially, designers are problem solvers because they work out how best to design something that will satisfy a need or purpose.

WHAT

What is the need the product must meet?

WHO

Who will use the product?

WHY

Why will people buy or use your design ahead of others?

HOW

How will people use it?

WHEN

When or how often will people buy or use your design?

RESULT

Function + Purpose + Style + Affordability = a well-designed product that is appealing to consumers

WHAT
I want a computer that's light, fast and has all the latest features. What are my choices?
WHO
This is exactly the colour and style I've been searching for. It's almost as if it was made for me!
?
WHY
How am I supposed to choose from all of these alternatives? All I want is something that will work and look nice.
HOW
It's a very interesting piece of technology, and I'm sure it has the latest features. But what exactly does it do?
WHEN
This is perfect! It'll look great on the kitchen bench, and we'll use it every day!

4 How to Become a Designer

First, think about what kind of design speciality you wish to pursue. Then, find out which school subjects you will need to have good grades in to apply for a TAFE course or university degree course. Research what kinds of design jobs are available, and what they involve.

A Graphic Designer

Graphic designers create visual designs and images. They use illustrations or photographs, different lettering styles, and a range of materials (such as paper, cloth or other media) in order to communicate a visual message. The end product of their designs might be books, advertisements or anything else that is meant to be seen by others.

Graphic design jobs for highly creative and practical designers are usually plentiful as the skills are transferable across many industries.

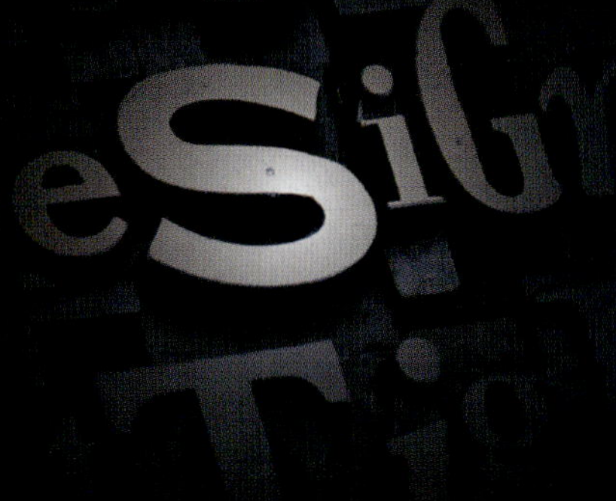

A Graphic Designer's Portfolio

Graphic designers specialise in using shape, colour, imagery, typography and space to present visual information in a way that aids communication.

Start a portfolio to showcase your designs. These must have maximum impact and include a range of visual communication pieces, for example, information leaflets, online advertisements, billboards, posters, product packaging, hard-copy books and ebooks.

TYPOGRAPHY

Typography is the art of choosing fonts and arranging lettering to achieve a desired visual effect.

5 Fashion Designing for Kids

Imagine you're thinking about becoming a designer of young children's clothing. Designers and clothing manufacturing companies know that they must design and make clothes for growing children that will be fun, practical and safe to wear. But, above all, they know that consumers want to buy kids' clothes at affordable prices because they will only be worn for a limited period of time.

Health and Safety

An important health-and-safety consideration when designing clothes for very young children is to use nonflammable fabric. Most clothes will include a label informing parents that the fabric is nonflammable or fire-resistant.

Fashion designs for kids are shown off at a fashion show in Spain.

A Fashion Designer's Attributes and Skills

Artistic Flair

Can create fresh ideas that are practical, functional and cost-effective to produce.

Innovation

Always keeps up to date with design trends and knowledge.

Listening Skills

Is a good listener when a brief is being explained.

Teamwork

Can work well in a team to collaborate on designs and accept constructive criticism of ideas as part of the development and improvement process.

Record Keeping

Maintains records of design progress, results and costs in a spreadsheet format.

Communication

Can present ideas in written and visual forms for customers, including company directors, retailers, other designers and marketing people.

DESIGN BRIEF: DESIGN A SUNHAT AND SUNGLASSES FOR A YOUNG GIRL

First design: Hat too big and heavy; oversized sunglasses. Revise design and try again. !

Attractive, brightly coloured items are displayed in a tidy way.

Revised design: Hat and sunglasses more in proportion to girl's face. Much better!

DESIGN BRIEF: DESIGN THE INTERIOR OF A CHILDREN'S CLOTHING STORE

6 Designing Ergonomic Furniture

Furniture designers need to design products with maximum impact to catch consumers' attention amidst a highly competitive market. Their furniture must meet safety standards, be easy to use, include ergonomic features for support and comfort, and be durable and stylish. A furniture manufacturing business will want its designers to follow a design brief and come up with designs that will be cost-effective and efficient to manufacture in terms of time, materials and resources.

Design an Ergonomic Desk and Chair for Kids

Think about how long you sit down every day. Research shows that most people are sitting for extended periods of time, and the longer we sit, the greater the impact on our posture and physical health. Ergonomic furniture is specially designed to be adjustable to suit the size of the person using it, so that they may sit without incurring any physical aches.

Laptop at eye-level to minimise neck strain while doing vital internet gaming research

Hollow round desk pillar, perfect size for storing leftover pizza

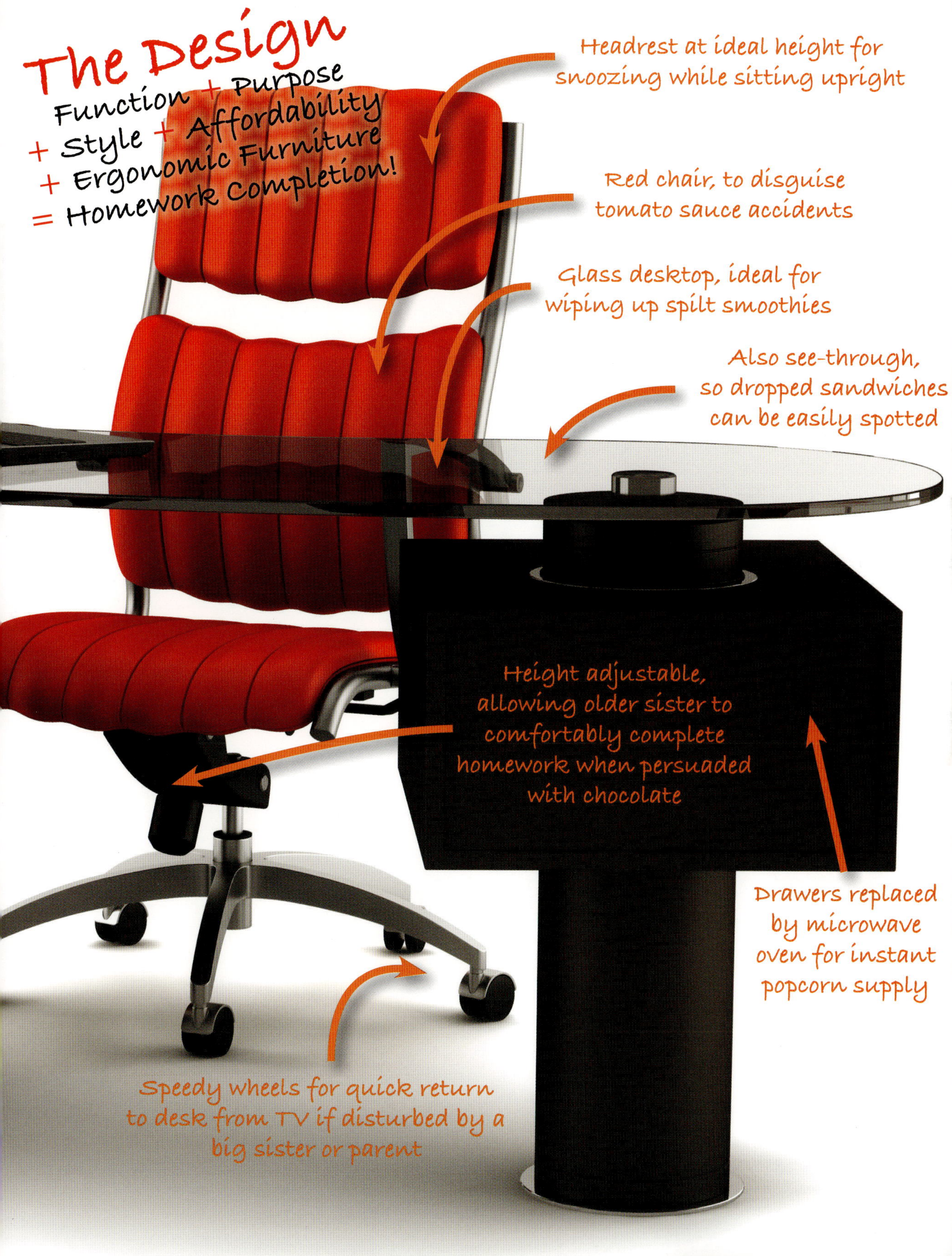
The Design
Function + Purpose
+ Style + Affordability
+ Ergonomic Furniture
= Homework Completion!
Headrest at ideal height for snoozing while sitting upright
Red chair, to disguise tomato sauce accidents
Glass desktop, ideal for wiping up spilt smoothies
Also see-through, so dropped sandwiches can be easily spotted
Height adjustable, allowing older sister to comfortably complete homework when persuaded with chocolate
Drawers replaced by microwave oven for instant popcorn supply
Speedy wheels for quick return to desk from TV if disturbed by a big sister or parent

More Designer Jobs

Industrial designers usually have an engineering background. They design manufactured objects, from small kitchen gadgets to massive structures and machinery. Small items are usually mass-produced, whereas fewer large machines will be produced. Safety is a critical factor in the design, especially for a kitchen gadget, such as a potato peeler, which is used by hands and fingers in a moving action.

Set designers will most likely have a background in theatre, television or film. Their role is to create memorable sets that support the action on TV or stage, or in the movies.

Landscape designers have a thorough knowledge of the best plants to grow in all kinds of climates and environments according to consumers' needs. They bring innovation to an outside environment when they combine nature with human-made structures.

Big machinery designers are industrial designers who specialise in designing big work machines, such as farming machinery and construction equipment.

Interior designers plan and design interior spaces, for example, homes, hotels and hospitals. Some interior designers specialise in one area of a building, such as bathrooms or kitchens. Various aspects of the interior design include lighting, furniture, artwork, floor coverings and paint colours.

Transportation designers, or **transportation engineers** as they are more commonly known, will usually have an industrial design qualification and may find themselves designing cars, trucks, buses, trains, ships, cruise ships and even hovercraft!

7 The Manual Toothbrush Is More Effective than the Electric Toothbrush!

Welcome to today's Dental Symposium. Technology has helped designers to create electric toothbrushes that clean teeth in any of the following ways: they may use a vibrating, rotating or oscillating motion, or they may clean teeth ultrasonically. But are any of these ways better than manually brushing teeth? Today's guests will tell you that the traditional manual toothbrush remains the best option for a number of reasons.

The Chairperson's Introduction

The manual toothbrush is an example of a perfect design. Although the materials used to construct toothbrushes have changed over time, this simple and effective oral hygiene tool has remained largely unchanged since it was first designed and used in China in the tenth century. Then, as now, a manual toothbrush solved the problem it was designed to address, met the needs of the user, and was simple and cost-effective.

A Dentist

To maintain oral hygiene, the teeth and areas around the gums must be kept clean. Otherwise, a film of bacteria called plaque will build up. As well as being unpleasant, plaque can hasten tooth decay and gum disease. The simplest and most effective way to keep bacteria and plaque from building up on teeth is to brush them regularly. Many approaches have been used in the past – such as chewing twigs or rubbing salty rags over teeth – but nothing works more effectively than a simple manual toothbrush. If it is used properly, a manual toothbrush will effectively keep teeth clean and gums healthy.

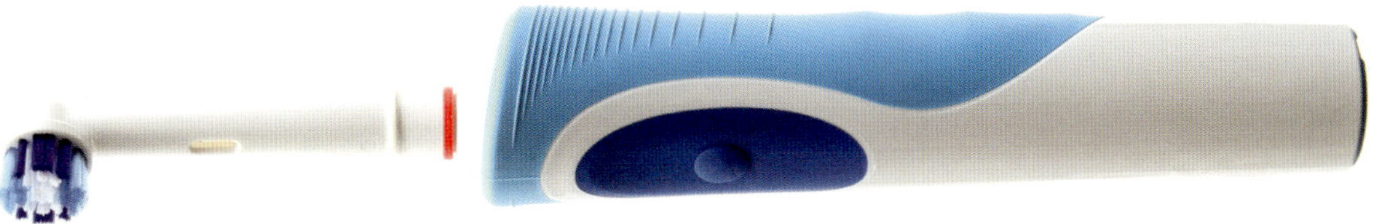

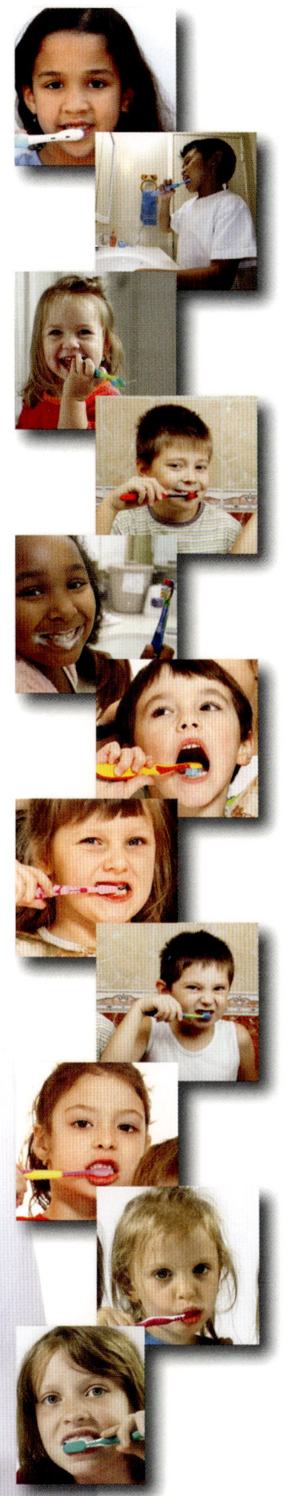

A Toothbrush Manufacturer

A good design should meet the needs of the user, and the manual toothbrush accomplishes this superbly. It is lightweight, easily manoeuvred around the mouth, can be easily gripped, comes in a range of attractive colours, requires little or no maintenance, will never break down or run flat, easily affordable to replace, and it would be hard to think of anything that is more portable.

A Dental Researcher

The manual toothbrush meets the needs of its users. This was proven in 2003, when the Massachusetts Institute of Technology carried out a survey asking participants to nominate the most useful thing in their lives. The majority of participants voted for the manual toothbrush as the number one thing that they could not do without. The toothbrush scored higher than cars, mobile phones and computers!

Even before manual toothbrushes started to be mass-produced in the late nineteenth century, there were few items that were simpler and more cost-effective to make. Toothbrushes in the nineteenth century were made from inexpensive and readily available materials, such as wood, bone and animal hairs. As materials improved in the first half of the twentieth century, plastic handles and nylon bristles replaced natural materials, and toothbrushes became even cheaper and more durable. As a result of these design enhancements, manual toothbrushes became even more fit for their purpose.

The Chairperson's Conclusion

The basic design of the manual toothbrush has been so effective that it remains in use after more than a thousand years. In all that time, it has maintained the oral hygiene of countless people. Twice a day, it meets virtually every requirement of its users, and there can be few, if any, other objects that can provide health care for weeks on end for only a few dollars. When combining the efficiency and low cost of a manual toothbrush, there don't seem to be any compelling reasons to replace it with an alternative!

HEALTH AND TECHNOLOGY FEATURE

WHY FLOSS, BRUSH and RINSE?

Bad dental health can lead to chronic health conditions. The best way for the government to prevent these health problems is to educate children about why they should have good dental healthcare routines every day. Two of the main culprits in our diet are processed sugar in foods and drinks, and acid-rich foods, for example, pineapple.

Medical scientists have discovered that the mouth can contain billions of bacteria, which can multiply very quickly! When bacteria is not removed through flossing, brushing and rinsing with water or mouthwash, dental health problems can occur, such as:

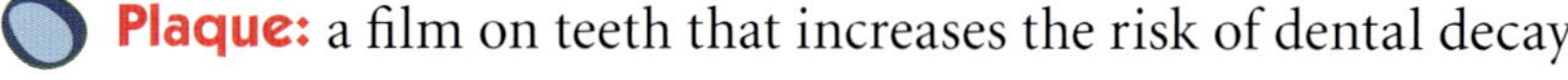

- **Plaque:** a film on teeth that increases the risk of dental decay
- **Gingivitis:** an inflammation of the gums that is the start of gum disease
- **Periodontitis:** an inflammation of the bones and tissues that provide support for the teeth.

FLOSS

BRUSH

RINSE

  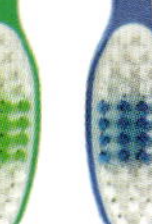     

DESIGN A DENTAL TOOL KIT

IMAGINE ...

Imagine that the government's health department has announced that it will fund a free Dental Tool Kit from its annual budget. The kit will contain a toothbrush, dental floss, toothpaste and a dental care brochure. The Dental Tool Kit will be available free for every six-year-old child at all primary schools on 12 September, which is World Oral Health Day.

WHY ...

One study revealed that many children still do not brush their teeth twice daily and do not know how best to brush and floss their teeth.

Not all families of young children can afford to pay for regular dental treatment and may not have access to dental education.

Design ideas: toothbrush, floss, toothpaste, brochure. Remember to include points below in brochure. Have ready by 12 September!!!

DENTAL CARE CHECKLIST

Eat Well: Consume a wide variety of healthy foods, and minimise the eating of foods with added sugar.

Drink Well: Drink sufficient water and minimise the consumption of drinks with added sugar.

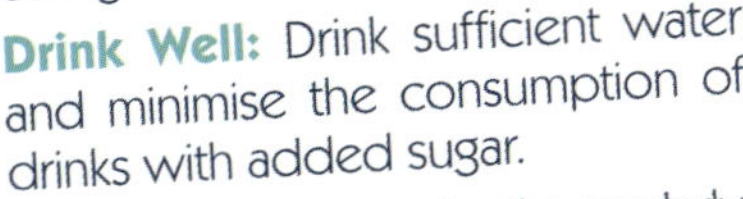

Keep Well: Visit the dentist regularly, don't wait until a problem occurs.

Play Well: Wear a protective mouthguard when taking part in sports, for example, football, or recreational activities, for example, skateboarding.

Clean Well: Brush and rinse morning and night, floss and rinse once a day, and rinse as often as you like!

Index

Glossary

design brief A written description given to the designer that outlines the purpose and desired characteristics of the product

durable Not easily worn out

ergonomic Designed to support a worker's body in their place of work, in a healthy way

manual Operated by hand

mass-produced Manufactured in large quantities using a mechanical process

nonflammable Not able to be set on fire

sustainable Able to be continued without hurting the environment or running out of natural resources

symposium A meeting to discuss a particular topic

unprocessed Still in its natural state, not treated or converted by any process